RECONSTRUCTING A RELATIONSHIP

MICAH CASTLE

To my beautiful wife, Nicole

CONTENT WARNING

This book contains scenes of rape and domestic violence. Read at your own discretion.

PART I

THE GAS STATION lights are harsh in the night. I wince as I pull under the metal canopy, parking at the nearest pump. I kill the car, grab my wallet on the dash, and get out. The tank lid creaks when it opens, and the cap's missin'. Years later, I still wonder where it is.

I feed the pump my card, shove the nozzle in, squeeze the handle.

"What's a pretty thing like you doing in the middle of the country?" a man's voice calls from across the lot.

I push a strand of blonde hair behind my ear, smile that stupid smile Drew loved, peer over the hood at the chubby man standin' next to a rusted green pick-up. His faded band t-shirt is far too tight, and the camo shorts are so long they almost touch his muddy boots. Why not wear pants at that point? Or are they pants, a size too small?

"Just drivin' around," I say. "I love backroads, but I must've not paid attention and ended up here."

He adjusts his short's lining, grins, smooths back his greasy hair. "Well, I know a thing or two about these roads. I can show you some that aren't even on the internet."

I glance at the belted cooler in the backseat, soon it'll be with my love. Wish I could be home sooner, but this one was out of state. Can't piss where I sleep.

"Miss?"

I look up and he's past the median. Hands in his pockets and I don't know if he's fiddlin' with his phone or what.

"No," I say, as the nozzle clicks. I pull out and shove it back into its cradle. No receipt. Slam the lid closed. "But thanks for the offer."

He stops between his truck and my sedan. Hands not moving in his pockets anymore. He shakes his head, mumbles somethin', grins. Starts forward again as though he's reworked his plan.

I get inside my car, throw the wallet on the passenger seat, start the engine. I put my belt on while he crosses the next median. This close I can smell what I imagine to be beer, chew, piss, or all three.

"But wait, miss, I know so many *cool* places—," he starts to say, leaning towards my car, but I press on the gas and skid out from the station. I don't intend to but I fishtail on the gravel before the road, and I wrench the wheel and straighten.

In the rearview, the man looks lonely. The only person at the station, lights casting a shadow across the pavement. Is he cryin'? Jesus.

"People out here are fuckin' weird," I mutter, and turn on the radio. Rock n' roll issues from the speakers.

I toss my keys on the counter, and heel the door closed as I carry the cooler to the basement. I set it down to pull out the free-standing freezer. If it weren't for the wheels I installed, it'd be impossible to move. Behind it is a steel door, which I unlock from keys clipped to my jeans. I pull it open, lean into the freezing darkness and flick on the lights.

"Honey, I'm home," I almost sing, takin' the cooler and closing the metal door behind me. Past hangin' plastic that for some reason is needed for a freezer, there's Drew, my love.

He's lying on the metal table, eyes closed, like always. His gray-blue skin looks good, and the sutures around his left elbow from my last visit are still keepin'. The others are fine, too. No reason to re-do them, thankfully. I remember the time they came undone on the back of his head, and his brain almost spilled out. Holy shit was I terrified I was goin' to lose him a second time.

I open the cooler awkwardly with one hand, toss the cover, and pull out the liver. It's like holdin' thawed chicken. Slippery, slimy, soft but solid.

I drop the cooler, and use my other hand to peel back his abdominal skin. Like the sutures, organs are doin' fine. Gallbladder—although he didn't need it, I want him to be the way he was. Kidneys. Stomach. Both intestines. Heart. Lungs. Check. Check. Check.

"Now," I mutter, leaning forward, placin' the liver under the lungs, above the gallbladder, "here it goes." I move it a bit until it slowly sinks in place, and wipe my hands on my jeans. Removing the scalpel from my back pocket, I carve a small symbol into the organ, matching the others and bones.

"Lookin' good, lookin' good." I stand back. The thick, wavy metallic symbols burnt into the table outlining him glean under the floodlight. Almost done. Still need a ribcage. Bladder. A left foot. And… That's all until he's back and we're together. No longer me, but him and I, *us*, even after death. Bless the books I found in those seedy, cellar shops. Wasn't much of a reader before this, but, shit, I am now.

I wipe the scalpel off on my thigh and toss it on the metal table to the side. Stare down at Drew for a moment, two. He's so fuckin' handsome, even with his new head. I grab the cooler and leave, switchin' off the lights on the way out.

THERE'S NOTHIN' like a smoothie in the dead of summer. Literally nothin'. Everything you love put into a blender and mixed together to create an amazing drink. Strawberries. Yogurt. Bananas. Fuck it, even blueberries and raspberries and cherries. I'm not picky. It's like Drew. All these parts from different places makin' one perfect thing.

The lights in the living room are still on, so I must've forgotten to turn them off when I left. I take a sip and sink into the old recliner I inherited from my father. I grab the remote from the coffee stand, switch on the TV.

"Obama's leading in the polls—"

Switch.

"Five Dollar Fo—"

Switch.

"In the arms of an—"

Switch.

"Yes!"

My favorite show. *Love & Lust of Sacred Heart.* Barry's makin' a move on Tiffany in the storage closet on the hospital's second floor, while her husband is makin' the same moves on Gregory in their own bed! Oh boy. Great writing. You love it when you see it.

I finish the smoothie and set the cup down. Although I love the show, I've seen this episode before. I sit back and let my mind wander.

The next goal is the ribcage. The bladder and foot can wait. Can probably get the two of them easily, but the ribcage will be tricky. Definitely will need someone for that. Can't take it and let them go.

Tap my fingers on my lap, start humming some unknown tune.

How far should I travel?

Don't think my cooler could fit one Drew's size. Might need to buy a new one...

Bones seem so easy but not as easy as organs. Throw them in and you're good to go. Have to clean bones... Shit. That's another thing. Need more beetles.

God why does it have to be fuckin' bugs? Wish I could use bleach.

So: get beetles, get bigger cooler, pick a town, a place, meander—no wait, rent a room, just in case—then meander, find someone and wham-bam thank you ma'am.

I grab my cup, go to take a drink—never mind, it's empty.

Damnit.

AFTER FILLING A BIG OL' bucket with beetles, leavin' it in the room with Drew, sealed of course, I drive two-hundred miles west to a small town called Nerwood. A half a mile long business district cuts through downtown, flanked by small, clustered shops, mostly shuttered with 'for rent' signs in the windows. Past downtown, gabled houses spread out in both directions until woods overtakes them.

It's quaint here. Nice. Has that small town after a recession vibe.

I drive until I find the Owl Inn. An old bar serving as a motel, I guess. Inside, I speak to an old broad with a tattoo of a flamin' heart on her right breast and pay for a seedy room in the back of the building. There's a bed with a moth-eaten blanket, scratchy pillow, an old 80s dresser, and a black-and-white tubed TV atop.

I don't bother leavin' anything there. I'm not stayin'. I'd rather sleep in the back of the sedan than get fleas or bed bugs. Renting's for looks.

Back in the car, I leave the inn and idly drive up and down streets, alleys, gravel roads. Not many people outside. I look at the sky and notice it's cloudy. Might storm soon. Works in my favor, really. Rain and thunder hide footsteps, washes away blood; almost does the job for me.

Eventually I park at a 7-11 and grab a blueberry slushy and a pack of Funyuns. Sittin' in the driver's seat, I slurp the slushy too fast and get a brain freeze. Hissing, I shove Funyuns into my mouth in the hopes it'll help. They don't.

People are pumpin' gas, and going into the station. Some are around Drew's size but they have to be nearly perfect. Can't be too big or too small. Drew wasn't a big guy, but wasn't tiny either. He had heft, the kind you loved to throw your arms around or be overwhelmed by behind closed doors.

God, I miss him.

Soon, Terry, soon.

A tall man gets out of a lifted truck and strides into the 7-11. He has the same build as Drew. Sort of. His gut peeks out from his flashy t-shirt, hangin' over his belted blue jeans, but it's not the meat I want.

I wait until he gets back in his vehicle and leaves, then I follow.

MY TEMPLES ARE POUNDIN' and I've been gnawin' on my bottom lip for what feels like hours. This dumb asshole hasn't stopped anywhere good. He went to a bar, to another gas station, to a house, then to another bar with some short man with big ears. I parked a few cars down, away from the street-light. The clouds must've been a false alarm because there hasn't been a drop of rain or clap of thunder.

I'm glad I don't need ice for this. It would've melted by now. At least the trunk is tarped, so I don't need a big ol' cooler.

I sit up as both men stumble out the bar. They laugh, holdin' each other, and grin like two buddies who just shared a woman. The big-eared man breaks away, stumbles, wavin', down the street. He must live close by. The man who has Drew's ribcage watches his friend leave, and fumbles with his keys he takes from his back pocket. He staggers, almost falls face first, but catches himself on his truck.

Damnit. Can't a girl get a break?

Like it's a big task, he finally gets behind the wheel, turns the ignition.

I'm not one for drunk drivin', but I have priorities. If he crashes, it makes my life a helluva lot easier.

His headlights wink on, he pulls out onto the road, and passes by. I'm on his ass a couple minutes later.

. . .

HE PULLS into a rutted road bordered by trees, and my sedan is rattlin' like a tin can as I try to keep my cheeks to the seat. The bumps and dips are hell. I bite the inside of my mouth, and blood coats my tongue.

"God damnit," I say like I'm deaf.

He turns into a dirt driveway. I stop before the drive, turn off the car. The only lights are the stars. No sounds but his engine cooling. His belching. His boots on the ground.

I silently unbelt, pull on rubber gloves, and remove the huntin' knife from the glovebox.

He's mumbling somethin'. Chuckles. I'm outside and tiptoein' around the corner, up the drive. A trailer stands a dozen yards away, no lights on. I pray there's no motion sensor lights. He's stumblin' towards home. Stops. Runs a hand through his hair. Farts.

Christ.

I move around his truck and to the front, crouch.

He bends over, hands on his knees. Heaves. Oh, I know that feelin'. Before I met Drew, used to love partyin' and drinkin' and bein' rowdy until my stomach turned upside down, and all that booze wanted back up.

Nothin' comes out of his mouth, and he slowly straightens. Dry ones are the worst. Know all about those, too.

Before he can move, I hurry behind him and ram the blade into his side. I twist the blade, crank it down, pivoting its point under his ribs, twistin' it again. He screams and sobs, flails his arms, tries to pull the knife out, push me away, but I'm too quick and small for him to grab. I yank the blade out, kneel, switch hands, and shove it into his other side. Repeat.

Bloods soaks his shirt, his jeans, spillin' in rivulets into the dirt. He spins with lifeless, heavy arms, and his knees give out.

I crouch over him. He's still breathin'. Have to give it to him, he's one tough asshole. His glossy eyes search for somethin', and he's mouthin' silent words.

"Sorry bud," I say. "But I have a man to take care of."

I double fist the knife and slash across his throat. His eyes widen, lets out a gasp, then he's gone from the world.

Should've brought a change of clothes, but luckily the long roads back to home are empty like the fields surrounding them. I'll wash at the next pit stop. I wish the trunk was big enough to fit the beetles. They could've done their job while I did mine, now there'll be more waitin' when I get back.

A familiar soft rock song plays from the radio, and nostalgia bites me in the ass. My focus is on the road, but can't help but turn the volume up and let my mind drift.

Drew was at one of my regular spots, Gort's Bar, and the way he looked that night was like a sucker punch. How do people describe love at first sight? How do people describe the feelin' they get when they meet their soulmate, that those before them meant jack-shit in comparison? It was that hard, that *deep*. Made my heart fuckin' jackhammer. I hadn't seen such a beautiful man in a long damn time, probably since my Pa. Those piercin' blue eyes, that full dark hair, those arms big enough to carry two of me around forever. I wanted—*needed*—him like nothin' else. There's a first time for everything.

I took the empty stool by him and soon we were a few shots in, and I was surprised he already started gettin' tanked. He had at least fifty pounds on me and six inches, but my love's a lightweight. The jukebox in the back played the song that fills my car now. It was late. We were the only two left, everyone filed out once the bartender hollered: "Last call!" But we stayed, we didn't want to go to another bar, we wanted to remain together, this undeniable, warm electricity passin' between us.

Though he slurred his words and his eyes were swimmin', I knew he wanted me, needed me. Our love was a match ignited. It was the first night we met but it felt like our hundredth.

"Wanna get out of here?" I said, takin' a final shot and slammin' it down.

He nearly fell off his seat, his grip slippin' from the counter. I caught him before he hit the floor. He mumbled somethin', but I heard: "Yes" somewhere in there. And, hell, he could barely sit straight. Doubt he could walk to the front door or make it to his car. So, maybe we wouldn't spend our first night fuckin' each other's brains out, but I would take care of him, nurse him, make sure he had a place to puke and sleep it off.

Even after the accident, I still do.

He can't live without me, and I can't survive without him.

In a gas station bathroom, the dim light flickerin', I wash my clothes the best I can in the stained sink. The water runs cold, the warm doesn't work.

The hand soap hardly does anythin' to the blood stains on my jeans, but at least it looks more like I spilled raspberry juice on myself than murdered someone. I rub my hands and arms with soap until they're raw, and stare into the grimy mirror.

My blonde hair needs to be washed, but in a ponytail the grease is hardly noticeable. The black bags under my bloodshot eyes are darker than I'd like, but being so close to bringin' back Drew, there's not much I can do. My cheeks are shallow, draggin' down the acne scars. I clench my teeth, and there's bits of Funyuns stuck between them. I try to scratch them out but they're fuckin' *in* there.

I shake my head. Doesn't matter. No one's goin' to see me anytime soon. I splash water over my face, run inside to grab a bag of snacks and extra-large coffee, and get back into the car, parked away from any light.

Thirty-two miles to go.

DAWN BREAKS like it did that one mornin'. Soft blue sky, orange-red horizon, the rays of light basking everythin' in gold. We watched them from my front porch back when I lived on a huge hill. Though Drew was still passed out, I had dragged him out with me, sat him down, let him lean against me as his drool soaked into my shirt. I thought the mornin' air would help. It probably did. As the sun rose and the mist coverin' the town slowly disappeared, he snored and said somethin'. Finally, he was waking.

With a sharp inhale, he rubbed his eyes and sat up. Blinked a few times. His green eyes seemed to glow in the sunlight. They were like shinin' emeralds, pools of green I wanted to drown in. He looked around, faced me and asked: "How'd I get here?"

"You don't remember?" I said, slidin' over a cup of coffee already made. I removed the saucer on top.

He picked it and smelled it.

"It's fresh," I said.

He shook his head. "I remember going to Gort's and ordering a drink…"

"Me comin' in?"

He nodded, took a sip. "Yeah. You ordered me…"

"Two shots."

He took another drink, a longer one. "Then, nothing. It's blank."

"Shots will do that to you."

He chuckled, smiled that dumb smile I love. "I guess so." He set the cup down, empty. "The funny thing is I can't remember your name either."

"Terry."

"Drew," he said, as though I didn't know.

"So Drew, what do you want to do today?"

"I don't know, I'm still pretty tir—"

I swerve to the right as a semi-truck storms past me with its horn blarin'. I start coughin' from inhaling so sharply. I drink the lukewarm coffee and blink away the sleepy tears.

"*Fuck,*" I spit. Stay with it Terry. Almost home. Another gas station's up ahead, and I decide to stop there. I'm quick. I can feel eyes on me. I'm too wound up from insomnia and caffeine. It feels like I'm walkin' on air, through water. Grab a new coffee, a Red Bull, and more snacks despite the grit coatin' already on my teeth, then I'm in front of the wheel, on the road, headin' home.

I ALMOST GOT STOPPED by the police when I got into town. The cop eyed me as I passed him, like he was searchin' for somethin' to pull me over for, but I looked normal, *seemed* normal, and then I turned the corner and was gone. I practically fell out of after I parked in my driveway. I forced my weighty legs to the trunk, poppin' it like lifting a boulder, and carried the bundled tarp inside.

I dropped the ribcage in the beetle bucket by Drew. Sealed it. He looked as wonderful as he did when I left. I trudged back upstairs and collapsed into the recliner.

I let the cushions mold to my settlin' body and close my eyes.

Another trip finished.

Onto the organs.

HE GETS INTO THE CAR, opens the door for me from the inside. Starts it, puts his hand on my thigh, and glances over his shoulder as he backs out. I put my hand on his. It's date day. His idea.

WE'RE LAUGHIN', stopped at an intersection. Other cars against each other in every lane. It's warm. His hand is higher up on my thigh, inchin' towards my crotch. A handsy man. Our song comes on the radio and he takes his hand off the wheel, reachin' for the volume.

. . .

I'M SCREAMIN'. He's screamin'. The semi is taking up the whole windshield before it explodes and glass sprays us. Doesn't stop. Keeps goin', barreling through the driver's side. Metal tears. Wrenches. Whines as it's ripped from the car.

Violently spinnin'. The world's upside down, right-side up, upside down... No breathin' or thinkin', just adrenaline and tearin' and airbags smashin' my nose and blood suffocating me.

I'm screamin' for Drew or I think I am, while I tilt and roll and—

I SHOOT UP, double over and vomit. My heart's in my throat and my head's hammering.

The words: "My fault" bubble in my thoughts. If we would've never left. Had a date night at home. He would still be here. We would still be as we were. But he was persistent. He wanted out, for once. A nice day out on the town. A movie. Dinner. Beers to cap off the night. And, he knew I couldn't say no to his dumb smile or green eyes or the way he ran his hand through his dark hair.

"Fuck…" I wipe the spit from my mouth. It's been a few hours, but I don't want to sleep anymore, so I pull myself from the recliner, avoid the vomit, and go into the kitchen.

AFTER CLEANIN' up the puke, and makin' a pot of coffee, I go to work.

I realize I was an idiot.

Stupid, Terry, stupid.

The way the ribcage is placed in the body makes it almost impossible to put it in right with the organs and things already there. Hours spent carefully removin' each one, puttin' the ribs in, markin' it with dozens of tiny symbols, and settin' the innards back in, placin' them perfectly as before.

A second pot of coffee's made.

After, I watch the news. No reports of a missin' man. No reports of a body bein' found without a ribcage. Nada. Nothin'. Zilch. Perfect.

I finally take a shower, lettin' the water stream over me until it cools. I crank the hot water to max to get lukewarm, and decide the bladder's next. Maybe get the foot at the same time, but I can't take or kill anyone for a while. Let any potential heat cool down. Two bodies with stolen parts would raise questions, even miles apart.

The water goes cold, and grumblin', I turn it off.

IN PAJAMA SHORTS and a tank top, my wet hair tied back, I decide it's a day off. My limbs are still heavy. Everythin' seems exhausting' to do. Eat. Drink. Piss. I deserve to play hooky anyway. Everyone does.

In the guest bedroom that would've been Drew's 'man cave' is where the books are stored. Shelves of different sizes and colors and age are against the walls, and either ham-fisted with books until they're pokin' out like zits or empty except for a couple lyin' flat on the bottom.

It's nuts to think I never owned a single book until Drew. Never cared to read or write, or, hell, learn another language, especially some obscure, dead one. Never really had the chance to. Was raised in a family of doers, not thinkers. Also, books aren't cheap. Not a poor man's game, like we were. But Drew makes me a better person. He makes me *want* to be a better person. At least I know he appreciates everythin' I do. Some lovers don't.

I grab a thick book from the tallest shelf. Can't remember if I started it, but I must've since there's a bookmark on page 1,192. I take it downstairs, pass through the afternoon sun comin' in through the windows, and out to the back porch. I sit on the plastic lawn chair, inhale the fresh air, open the book, and begin.

BY MID-AFTERNOON, THE HEAT'S SWELLIN', and I'm inside preparing lunch. Newspapers and open notebooks are spread out over the vinyl table. The closed book sits on the counter. The AC in the livin' room window hums, spits, hums again. I sit, and take a mouthful of pepperoni and provolone sandwich while I scan the papers again.

There's no reports of a missin' man. I'm in the clear. Either the guy was a nobody or the body hasn't been found yet. Either way, if it's not on the news the next day, typically I'm good to move on.

Foot… foot… foot…

I use a red marker to circle potential spots. *Hospital* this, *Medical Center* that, *Tissue Storage*, etcetera.

I finish the sandwich, mark one last hospital a hundred-and-fifty miles away, and sit back, sighin', wipin' the sweat from my forehead. It was meant to be my day off, but here I am, workin' myself ragged again. I cap the marker and toss it on the table, go out the livin' room, and bask in the AC.

I'M LEAVIN' tomorrow for *Canetown Memorial.* Hundred-and-seventy-five miles out.

I just want Drew back. I want this shit to be done, and we can continue our lives as it was. I stand over him, holdin' his cold hand. Tears are comin'. A pit forms in my chest, and it's not heartburn. It's a hole made when the accident happened, and only he can fill it.

HUNDRED-TWENTY-SOMETHING MILES DOWN, fifty-ish to go. Chud's Diner is a quaint place. Chrome seatin', checkered linoleum floors, curved ceilin' painted with scenery from the sixties, a jukebox plays a dance number that maybe my mother would've known. I knock back a mint and chip milkshake, a double-stacked hamburger, and a side of fries.

"Want anything else, miss?" an old waitress asks.

"A coffee to go, please."

"On it," she says and clomps in high heels back behind the counter.

The bell above the door jingles when a couple enters and goes straight for a booth across the diner. Their hands intertwine on the table, as they smirk and giggle and make goo-goo eyes that I'm sure are x-rayin' through clothes. They'll order a shake with two straws. They'll share a plate of fries. They'll go back to their car and find an empty spot in a field somewhere and have at it in the backseat, or pop open the trunk and let the world see what their parents' gave them. To be in love; to be young. All fun and freedom and fuckin'.

I shake my head. Gotta' focus on the plan.

Rent a room somewhere, anywhere, in town.

Scope out the hospital for a couple days. Find out when or how they dump toxic materials.

Either seduce the garbage man or an orderly or whoever brings them out and disposes them.

Or steal it, if I have to.

Then home. No buts. No killin'. No blood. In and out.

The old waitress sets a strawberry shake on the couples' table, jabs two straws in, then walks over and hands me my coffee.

"Thanks," I say, but she doesn't reply. I slap down a twenty and leave before the couple begins their drink.

CANETOWN MEMORIAL IS A BIG, gray square building that towers over the parkin' lot surrounding it. Hell, it towers over the road and the second lot across a stretch of grass. People in scrubs come in and out of the front slidin' double doors, others stand around the ER doorway smokin' cigarettes. Trees dot grass here and there, breakin' up the flat, tarmac sea.

It reminds me of the hospital they took us to after the accident. Not shabby but not quite extravagant. A hospital that serves its purpose. Nothin' flashy like walls of windows or a Starbucks inside or other fancy shit. Bare rooms and doctors and nurses and drugs and death; lots of death.

I stretch my legs in the secondary lot across the road. I bend over, touch my toes, bend to the left, right, back. My hips and shoulders pop as I rotate them.

Driving for hours is awful.

My body revolts but I get back inside.

THE BACK IS about the same as the front, except a steel fence with barbed wire circling around the top blocks off a large portion of the lot. Inside are two big green dumpsters. Sliding doors nearby, I imagine, lead to the basement, where they cremate limbs and bones and other shit you can't throw away. There's two cameras above the doors, slowly movin' back and forth. I imagine there's more inside, too.

I turn off the engine, lean the seat back and close my eyes.

Now to be here when they do trash. Typically happens in the dead of night or early mornin', but I don't want to take any chances.

I must be exhausted because sleep comes fast.

FLASHES OF LIGHT. LOOMIN' people. Somethin's strapped over my face and air floods my nose. I can breathe through one nostril. Blood clogs the other. Smeary faces in silvery fog hover over me. Are my fingers still there? I can't tell if I'm movin' them or not...

"Drew" I mouth. "Where's Drew?" Mumblin', soundin' like gibberish...

"It'll be fine, miss," I hear. "Everything will be OK."

HALLWAYS and bright lights and softly colored wallpaper and big doors open, close, open, close. People talk with jumbled mishmash, not words. Eye. See. You. Eye. See. You. They repeat. What the hell do they mean? See what? See me? It's like fumblin' in the dark of my mind, then I'm tumblin' down stairs.

THE ROOM REEKS of bleach and my grandmother. The scratchy blanket and hard pillow are welcome. Somethin' cold trickles into my arm, pools in my chest. The chair by the bed is empty as the room. People in colored clothes pass by the open door. Finally, I feel my fingers, and there's a plastic thing in my palm.

I press the button atop.

A HORN BLARES and I jolt awake, wipe the drool from my cheek. The fence is open and there's a dump truck backed up inside. I don't know what time it is, but it's almost dawn. The sodium lamps give off a dull orange glow, but are washin' out as the sky lightens. A stocky man wearin' a reflective yellow vest stands by the truck's rear, holdin' down a lever as the dumpster is lifted by the truck's mechanical arms and dumped into the back.

Once he's done, they empty the other dumpster, then the man gets into the truck and it drives off. One. Two. Three. Four. Five—the gate starts to close—Six. Seven. Eight, it closes. Eight seconds I have to get in.

There's still Pepsi left in the bottle, and I gulp it down, grimacin'. I miss my smoothies. Rollin' onto my side, I go back to sleep.

AFTER RENTIN' a room at Motel 11-11, showerin', and grabbin' breakfast from a convenience store, I'm back in the sedan at the hospital around nine in the mornin'. I chomp down the egg-and-turkey sausage sandwich, sip from my coffee, and watch people move in and out of the front doorway.

Again, I go over the plan.

Get inside and go to the basement. Figure out the layout and where the freezer is, or crematory, or morgue; anywhere that things are stored after removal. Find out who runs the show and either seduce them—thank the Lord that Drew isn't alive to see me doin' that to another man—or take care of them, steal their keys, and get out.

No matter how temptin' it is, today's not the day for the steal. Today's for plannin'. No action. I wonder briefly if I should've just knocked someone out and sawed off their foot, but quickly scold myself. Can't do that, Terry. Two bodies in one month may raise questions. A foot stolen from a corpse at a hospital would be a tiny blip on the police's radar. They were already dead anyways, so who cares?

I finish my food and toss the wrapper in the backseat. I chug the rest of the drink, burnin' my tongue.

"Damnit," I spit.

No one paid attention to me passin' through the lobby, or in the elevator, or in the basement. Everyone is payin' attention to other things like notebooks and tablets and talkin' to one another. Oddly, not so much the patients. It's colder down here and I regret not wearin' more than a tank top. Nothin' hangs on the white cement walls, and the light gleans off the polished floor.

I try to follow the signs casually, like I'm late for an appointment. So many arrows and departments and room numbers, I have no fuckin' clue where to go or where to start, so I follow the yellow paint on the ground until it brings me to another sign a couple hallways and turns later.

"Radio… Nope.

"Laund… Nope.

"Neuro… Nope.

"Mortuary… Bingo." I whisper to myself. It has a green dot next to its name, so I follow the green strip all the way to a part of the basement that feels empty. No one's about, not a single medical staff. There's a set of double doors blockin' the way, and a big bald man sits at a steel desk in front of it. He's readin' a paperback that's too small for his hands.

OK, so… Seduction? Because I can't take this guy down.

My hair's dry and frizzy, so I tie it back. I push down the wrinkles of my tank top, adjust it to maximize the little cleavage I have, and hike up my jeans until I can feel them cup the underside of my ass. Probably should've cleaned my shoes, but too late for that.

I casually walk to the desk, lean against it with my hip, poppin' the other out a little. Seen younger girls do this in photos. Men seem to dig it. Fuckin' weird to me, but whatever.

"Hello," I say. "Do you work in the mortuary?"

He looks up from his book, inspects me from waist to face, and closes the paperback. "Yeah," he says with a flat voice. "With Joe," he thumbs the door. "But, usually he works the evening shift."

"Oh, nice. What's your name?"

He runs his palm over his scalp, points to his name tag. "Jason."

"Oh, Jason—I had a brother with that name…" I blink rapidly, give a heavy exhale. "Until he… Until he…"

Jason's eyes widen, and he stands. "Are you OK?"

I want to laugh at how ridiculous this is, but I force myself to stay in character. Actors have it *rough*. I narrow my shoulders, poke out my chest. He steals a peek at my cleavage, the rim of the light blue bra raisin' over my top, then his eyes lock onto mine. "He died. Car crash. I was… I was told he was brought to this hospital, that he was still down here."

"I'm so sorry, miss," he says, shakin' his head. "What's his last name? I can check." He picks up the tablet from the desk.

"Wiltbell. Jason Wiltbell."

I come around the desk as he searches the list, standin' against him, tryin' my best to press my chest against his doughy arm. "So many names," I say as though I'm dazed. "Are these all the people that died?"

He glances at me, my chest, back to the paper. Nods. "Uh huh." He flips the paper over the top, goes through another.

"Isn't it…" I bite my lower lip, force down a laugh. "Isn't it *scary* workin' here?"

I sniffle and wipe my eyes. He finishes the list. "Sometimes, but you have to deal with it; it's a part of the job. But, miss, he's not here." He turns to me, steps back. "Do you think you might have the wrong hospital? There's a few in the county."

I cross my arms, perch the babes on top. "No, I'm sure they said Canetown Memorial… Would you mind checkin' them? Maybe he's here, but not on the list."

He debates with himself for a moment, two, starin' blankly at poor little ol' me. "Yeah, I can do that—"

"Can I come with you?"

"No, miss—"

"But it's so scary here, and I don't want to be alone…"

He looks through the window in the door, down the hallway, back to me. "Please don't leave my side, please miss. This isn't a place for non-medical staff."

"I wouldn't dream of it, *Jason*," I say.

HE TOLD me to stand by the doorway as he looked over the small tags on the square metal cubbies coverin' the whole wall, but I stayed close. He hasn't complained. There's a counter along the far wall with a sink, boxes of medical gloves, tools, a big ass thing of hand soap, and glass cabinets above it. A couple steel tables under enormous, coned lights make up the rest of the room.

Coldness radiates from the metal doors, and now I'm not holdin' myself for show, because I'm fuckin' *freezing*. I scan the name tags, and find a Jason Walterbox. He'll be my brother. We reach the end of the wall.

"He's not here, miss," he says. "Are you sure he's here? You said Jason Wiltbell, right?"

I shake my head. "No, Jason *Walterbox*. My brother's name is Walterbox, not Wiltbell." I pray this works. I pray he seems as dumb as he looks. I shiver and the ladies jiggle a little. God this is stupid. I'm already way off plan and makin' everythin' up as I go. I just needed the keys but now I'm convincin' this guy that what he heard only ten minutes ago was somethin' else. And, he's sayin' nothing as he tries to figure out if I'm lyin' or not.

"Walterbox..." he mumbles.

I nod. "Yeah. I think I saw him around here." I point to one of the doors behind me.

Jason walks past me to it, reads the label. "This must be him. Sorry for the mix-up."

"No problem, it must be hard to keep track of everythin' here. Looks like you do all the heavy liftin'."

He smirks. "I do, but I manage."

"With those arms, you must." I smile. Christ...

He glances at his arms, and must flex because his arm wiggles.

"Oh, wow," I say. What the hell did I get myself into?

He realizes where we're at and stops grinnin'. "Okay, miss. Are you sure you want to see him?"

"Absolutely."

He undoes the latch, and opens the door. Cold mist spills out. I stand behind him as he pulls the bed out. A white sheet covers Jason's body, except for his blue-gray head.

"Oh!" I say. "Jason!" I force tears and stare at this stranger with short-cropped gray hair, a beak nose, and tiny lips. The other Jason comes up behind me, and before he can say somethin', I spin and bury my face into his man tits, wrappin' my arms around his bulgin' waist. I fake sob as he embraces me. It's like a fleshy cocoon. A life-sized teddy bear filled with gelatin. I can understand chubby chasers a little more.

He rubs my back, whisperin': "It'll be okay, miss. Everything will be okay."

I move my hand down his side, stop at his hip. I don't know if it's candy bar or what, but somethin' solid is pressin' against me.

Have to do what I have to do for Drew.

"I miss him," I say, my voice muffled against his chest. "We were so close."

My hand moves again, towards his front pocket. I have no idea how he doesn't feel me or notice. Maybe someone this size can't? Like livin' in the US and not feelin' an earthquake in China? Who knows?

"I understand, I understand," he says. "I had a brother who died in the war. We were close, too."

His pocket's empty. Fuck. I remove my hand and let it rest on his hip, while I try the other pocket with the opposite hand. The solid thing pressin' against me definitely ain't no fuckin' chocolate.

"What happened to him?"

Slip my hand in, feel a keyring.

"His convoy was blown up making a gasoline run. Nothing left but shrapnel."

I tug the ring, cup them, and slowly move my hand out. I look up at him and he's actually cryin', too. I sniffle and he looks down, leans in, and his lips meet mine. I wrap my arms around his neck, pressin' him close. His tongue slips into my mouth, rovin' around my teeth, pryin' between them like floss. This is fuckin' gross.

Whatever. Get this over with. I pass them to my right hand, slide 'em into my back pocket, and bring my hand back. God I hope they're worth it.

Our lips part, though he's tryin' to lick my tonsils.

"I'm sorry!" I say, steppin' back. "I didn't mean to. I—"

"It's okay," he reaches for me, but I move away. "It's meant to be. Don't you believe in fate?"

Seriously?

I beeline to the door. "I'm sorry but I can't. I... You're a kind man, and you've let me see my brother for the last time before he's buried and I'm grateful but… Not this, I'm not like that."

"But wait—" Desperation in his voice. A hard-on pokin' against his khakis. I'm out of the room before he can finish. Down the hallway, out the double doors to the elevator, to the lobby and out the front doors, and crossin' the lot to my car.

I need toothpaste. Mouth wash. Fuckin' acid.

IN MY ESCAPE, I didn't think to check where the door from the dumpsters to the mortuary was, so I'm sittin' in my car with keys that might not even help. The plan went to shit. I went to shit. Lost in a moment of actin' and BS. I groan and hit the steering wheel.

Okay. Okay. Get it together Terry. The finish line is right there.

The door has to lead there somehow. Why wouldn't it? Like puttin' your garbage can near the back door, so you don't have to go far to take it out. But it still could go somewhere else.

I grumble.

I'm goin' to have to play it by ear. Don't like doin' it, but it is what it is. Drew needs me.

I PARKED CLOSE to the gate before daybreak, hiding in the backseat, gloves, and ski-mask on, holdin' a piss-filled soda bottle. As soon as the dump truck left, I rushed out of the car, almost fallin' on my face, and sprinted between the narrowin' gap of the closin' fence. I spun around and set the bottle next to the fence. The gate stopped against it.

Hospital must've cut the budget for this because the gate didn't bother to try to push through. I felt accomplished for a moment, before runnin' to the double doors that slid open after I pressed a small card on the keyring to a black scanner on the wall.

A hallway led to large, closed doors, a huge elevator to the left, and a closed office or somethin' to the right. I took the elevator to the basement and prayed it didn't come out by anyone, especially Jason.

Relief washed over me when it opened directly before an office that I unlocked, which connected to the morgue. Steel countertop with papers and a computer, medical tools, and objects; a cabinet above filled with other odds and ends I didn't bother to look at, and another big, locked steel door in the back wall.

I peeked into the morgue. Empty. Then, went straight to good ol' Jason Walterbox, undid the latch and pulled him out. I threw off the sheet from his feet and wham, there it was: Drew's right foot.

I rushed to the tools, opened drawers and cabinets and other cubbies until I found a slick-ass hand saw. It must've been brand new, right from the rack. The overhead lights reflected off its stainless surface.

Back to the job, Terry.

I always thought that cuttin' through bone was difficult, that it was like slicin' through stone, but maybe Jason had been too cold for a while or maybe he wasn't a big milk drinker when he was alive, but the bone crumbled easily and soon the saw went through.

I forgot to bring a bag to carry it in.

"Fuck…"

I searched the room but only came away with an extra-large sized medical glove. I shoved the foot in there enough so I could carry it without touchin' it. Great. Wonderful. I left the saw on the bed with one-foot Jason, and bolted back into the office… Stopped.

I noticed the large metal door radiated cold, like the morgue's. Was God lookin' down on me? Had Christmas come early?

I fumbled with the keys with one hand and undid the lock, wrenched it open and holy *shit* it was an organ storage. I almost pissed my pants from excitement.

Inside, passin' through chilly fog, I inspected the wide variety of jars set on metal shelves. Big, small, huge, enormous. All filled with mostly yellow, light yellow, brown, and dark brown liquids. All containin' beautiful organs. Brains and lungs and pancreases and livers—if I found this place when I started, I would've been done a helluva lot sooner.

At the end of one shelf, at the bottom, floated a bladder in yellow fluid. It looked fine. No bumps or bruises, nothin' that would fuck up what I gotta do.

I scooped it into my other arm and got out of there, heelin' the door closed.

From the office to the elevator, from the elevator to outside, passed the dumpsters, side-steppin' through the gap in the gate, kickin' away the bottle to allow it to close; then jumpin' in the driver's seat, settin' everythin' on the passenger side, rippin' off the gloves and mask, and gettin' the fuck out of dodge.

. . .

My nerves are still on fire. I want to dance and sing and holler out the window goin' a hundred down the freeway. My fingers and toes are tinglin', my fun parts, too. The cooler in the back is jam-packed with my rewards. Rewards. Plural. Two. Goddamn! Drew will be back sooner than expected. I look in the rearview mirror, give a big smile, showin' yellowed teeth; pull down the dark bags under my bloodshot eyes.

I may wait until I can clean up before the big day. Don't want him seein' me at my worst. The last time he saw me was before the accident.

The grasslands surroundin' the road blur past. The sun's risin', castin' warmth.

It feels like the best day of my life.

I'm home. No stops. My feet feel somehow lighter not drivin', my right foot wantin' to press down on the ground. I carry the cooler to Drew. Though I haven't slept in what feels like weeks, I'm wired, bouncy, almost to the point of annoyance. I scar the foot with the symbols, place it to his ankle. Notice it's a bit shorter than his left, but I can fix that with shoe inserts or somethin'. Mark his bladder, set it on top of the end of the large intestines, above the asshole he won't use.

I stand back. Inspect.

"Fuckin' wonderful." It's perfect. He's perfect. I want to finish but exhaustion suddenly suffocates me, and sweet Jesus I nearly collapse right there. I leave Drew and go upstairs, crumble into the recliner.

"He's gone," White Coat says, like he's recitin' the weather. "He died on impact."

He vanishes into smoke.

Nothingness unlike the pain meds washes over me. My brain's tangled. Thoughts—fury, hurt, hate—all knotted together. Millions of criss-crossin' strands of yarn, all screamin'.

Impossible. A man like that doesn't just die. I refuse. Refuse. My hands are fists, my stomach like my brain; sweat like a too-tight bathing suit.

.   .   .

NIGHT. Absent nurses. Coldness seeps through my socks. Hallway empty, quiet. Down, down the emergency stairs. Down, down to the basement. A blue man passes the narrow window, then gone. I crabwalk out. Down, down to the morgue door.

ANDREW ZURASKY. Say his name aloud. Open the door, pull out the bed, revealin' my love. Beautiful. Skin cold. Hair patchy, dry. Eyes gone. Lips melted. Nose mangled. Teeth shattered. Cheeks torn. A maw by his ear, gray-blue inside. What makes him, him.

Not removed, yet.

SPRINTIN'. Alarms blare. Don't have his body but mind. Feet slappin' concrete. Lungs on fire. Cold air bitin' my chest. I can't stop. Refuse. Refuse. Refuse. He belongs with me. He must return, somehow, someway. Boundless love. A forest in the dark. Pass brush, trees. Ankle-deep mud and knee-high creeks. Pavement replaces earth. Tires screech. Blindin' lights.

"YOU OKAY MISS?" Flannel Shirt says. "Need help?" Drew beneath my gown.

Yes. Help. Please.

"Oh, okay, miss, you can sit up front."

I sit in the back, Drew on my lap.

Trees smear. Countryside replaces them. Night becomes dawn. Highway appears. Flannel Shirt talks and I respond.

A twenty in my hand, a motel behind me, the car disappearin' into the horizon—

IT'S NIGHT, or still is night. I don't know when I passed out. My joints ache when I stand, and I have to stretch my legs a bit to wake them. I half-limp, half-stumble into the kitchen, get coffee goin', and plop down into a chair. Elbows on the table, face in hands. I rub the drowsiness away like its dirt as the smell of hazelnut fills the room.

Fuck I feel awful. Haven't felt like this since my first kegger. So many drinks my blood was beer and my piss liquor.

The pot hisses and I lurch to the counter, fill up the biggest mug I can find, and sit right back down and let the steam and aroma waft over me, fill my nose. Wait until it cools because burnin' your tongue is a bitch. Take a tiny sip. Oh sweet mother of Mary it's delicious. It grows in my chest. It soaks into my stomach. I'm a garden and it's the rain.

"Okay…" I say, gravely, soundin' like my Ma. "Plan. What's the plan, Terry?"

Isn't it obvious?

Drew. Bring Drew back. Get the room right. Get the books. Get the supplies and shave and lotion and wear that thing he loves because who fuckin' knows. Gone that long, he may want a happy surprise when he first comes to.

But first…

I drink more coffee.

Drew's room is gloomy, only the candlelight lets me read the big old book open in my hands. I hope the snakin' symbols around the candles, the walls, and the floor that connect to others around Drew are right. I'm no artist, and they are weirdly shaped and twistin'. Who comes up with them? Why can't they be regular-ass squares or triangles? Or…

Terry! Back on track.

Drew is stitched and sealed, almost as beautiful as he was that day at the bar. Wish his head hadn't cracked like an egg, those damn eyes. My clothes are tighter than I remember. Must've gained some weight since I bought them. He won't mind, more to love and all that.

A big chunk of purple crystal dangles above the table, strung up around the light. A silver vein burrows through it, pokes out the bottom with little nubs. I don't recall where I got it, but it did cost a damn fortune.

Butterflies flutter in my chest, hammers pound on my temples. I'm lightheaded. Feels like undressin' for a guy for the first time. Feels like startin' high school. Feels like lookin' down the barrel of my Pa's rifle after I sassed him.

Exhale. Inhale. Breath…

I focus on the pages, the ugly words that are like Vaseline in my mouth. I recite them the best I can manage but it's like Bit-o-Honey between my teeth, like straight oil on my tongue, like bile comin' up my throat. I force it out. My knees ache, my fingers go cold. The crystal swings from Drew's feet to his head, back again, like a pendulum. There's a whooshin' noise blowin' from somewhere, and I'm scared whatever's runnin' the show can't hear me, so I start shoutin'.

The silver vein glows red-hot and the nubs eject thick strands of melted metal over Drew, onto the symbols that rattle, shiver. Their glow matches the vein. I'm not sure if it's the room or me but suddenly it's middle-of-summer humid. Sweat stains the pages, soaks my clothes, builds between tits and ass cheeks.

My lungs work double-time between heavy words.

The crystal stops right above Drew and explodes with light, blinding me, burning my skin. I drop the book, turn away, closing my eyes as I hide my face in my arms. The whooshin' becomes churnin' milk and swampy gurglin' shrieks all around me—

PART II

Searing air burns my lungs. Whiteness stings my eyes. Am I in the hospital? How long have I been out? I cough and dislodge something phlegmy, wipe it on my thigh—Have I gained weight? I feel fatter, doughier… And, where are my clothes? I run my hand over my chest and stomach, the other down my legs, my groin. Everything's there but feels different, *off*, like I'm wearing clothes backwards. A strange discomfort.

The light darkens. Candles are placed around a square room, a few unlit, smoke slithering from burnt wicks. A big, purple crystal hangs above me, sizzling and steaming. What the hell are these symbols everywhere? Why am I on a metal table? Why is it so *damn* cold?

No way…

Terry stands in front of hanging plastic sheets, a huge black book on the ground, wearing a too-tight frayed black, lacy teddy. Hair tied up with mascara running down her face.

She lived?

She's alive?

Fuck. Shit. No, no, no. I swing my legs off the table and plant my feet on the floor. Try to put weight on them but it's like they're asleep, like I haven't used them for months. I fumble forward, try to grab something to stop myself but there's nothing to hold. I crash into Terry, sending her to the floor. I hear her head crack against the cement.

Hopefully, that'll do it. Doubtful if a semi-truck couldn't.

I stumble through the sheets and smash against a closed steel door. I hold onto it for dear life with one hand, search for a handle or knob with the other.

A latch. I yank it down, and fall face-first onto a basement floor, knocking the air out of me.

"Drew?" Terry groggily calls from behind. "Baby?"

My legs won't move and I'm straining to drag myself forward. My arms are weaker, lighter. My fingers are half-numb. Have to close the door. Lock it. Get to the stairs and get out of here. Call the police. Call my parents.

Help. I need help!

"What're you doin' honey?"

I look over my shoulder. She stands over my legs, her hands on her hips. One of her breasts popped out. There's red marks on her chest and arms. I open my lips to scream but a deaf gurgle escapes me. I want to cry but no tears come.

What's wrong with me?

"Don't tucker yourself out yet, dear," she says, walking around and kneeling in front of me. "There's so much to do." She starts to cry, and backhands her eyes. "It's been so long, Drew..." She rubs my cheek, holds my chin up. "I've missed you so fuckin' much."

She presses her lips to mine and I want to vomit. Then—

Flashes of consciousness.

Terry riding me, writhing, her head back, hair undone.

Darkness.

Terry gasping, moaning.

Darkness.

I feel nothing, literally. My groin isn't there, as though it's elsewhere, somehow.

Darkness.

Something *must* be there because she's gyrating faster.

Darkness.

She digs her nails into my chest as she leans forward, her mouth gaping, eyes rolling into the back of her skull.

Darkness.

She laughs, smiles.

Darkness.

She lies on top of me, her finger twirling around my nipple. "Was it as good for you as it was for me, Drew?"

I want to revolt and run. I want to berate her but only more gurgles come out.

"Oh honey," she says. "Don't bother. A tongue isn't somethin' you needed. Our love doesn't need words."

Something I didn't need?

What is she talking about?

I go to move my tongue around my mouth, but it's missing. Like my groin, there's an emptiness. I feel my tongue but at the same time I don't. A lingering ghost between my teeth. I start to cry but, again, there's no goddamn tears.

Why aren't there tears?

Why don't I have a tongue?

What happened to me?

Terry guides me upstairs to the kitchen. It takes a while because I can't shake this weird limp. Dirty dishes pile high in the sink, and a layer of grime covers the countertop. I don't want to sit, but she pushes me down by my shoulders. I'm still nude and the hard seat digs into my ass.

"What do you want for your first meal?" She walks around the table to the fridge. Opens and leans into it. She's still wearing the teddy and its taut between her flat ass. I hold back a gag. "I can make you some pancakes, cereal, mash potatoes, …" Her voice fades as I glance around, searching for anything to help.

No knives, but some may be in the dirty dishes. No forks or spoons or anything that could be used as a weapon. Through the window above the sink, it's night or early morning, I can't really tell from this angle. The padlock on the backdoor is turned, and down the hallway the front door seems the same. A room offshoots the hall.

I want to break down and sob.

How could I have ended up back with her?

Again?

After I was so close to getting away.

Honestly believed the date day was the answer. The dumb bitch even let me drive. I wish that trucker…

"Drew? Drew? You listenin' to me?"

I shake my head, face her. She's in front of the open fridge, a box of milk in one hand, an egg in the other. "What the hell do you want to eat?"

I'm not hungry. I can't feel my stomach like I used to. Wasn't a big eater then, and it seems that little bit of hunger is gone. But, I'm cold, freezing.

I shrug and point to my chest, my legs, draw a shirt and pants with my finger. It takes her a second to understand. "Oh…" Nods. "Come with me."

She tosses the food back in the fridge, I hear the egg break, and grabs my hand. Drags me down the hallway—the front door *is* locked—and upstairs.

As she rummages in her bedroom closet, I peer out the window. We're not in the same house she used to live in. Not on top of that hill. She couldn't afford that place anymore, I guess. There's a patchy front yard with a steel fence, a cracked sidewalk, a road riddled with pot-holes, and an empty lot and a couple dilapidated houses. We must be on the poor side of town— what town, I have no idea.

"Here we go!" she says, presenting a frayed long black t-shirt, faded jeans, and a crumpled pair of yellowed underwear. I don't bother wondering whose they were.

I point to my feet.

She tosses me the clothes, and turns back to the closet.

I slide on the shirt, grimacing as I pull up the underwear, then the jeans. Everything's scratchy. I want to tear them off but the warmth outweighs my disgust.

Two mismatched socks hit my chest, fall to the floor.

"Here you go."

I bend over and slip them on. Much better. When I straighten she's staring at me from across the room, nude. I don't understand what it is exactly, but she's vile. Almost all women have some slight appeal when nude, not specifically me, to anyone. Everyone can find someone who loves them, finds them attractive, fits together like two puzzle pieces… But I can't fathom who would enjoy Terry's saggy body. It's like she aged rapidly and her body couldn't keep up. I briefly wonder if she does hard drugs.

"Like what you see?"

I force a nod.

"Wanna go again?" she grins.

I shake my head, point to my groin, mouth: "Sore."

"Maybe tomorrow," she mutters, and pulls out some clothes from the closet. She throws on a tank top and low-riding jeans. She crosses the room, wraps her arms around me, pulls me in. "I want to show you some-thin', Drew. I want to show you how much I love you."

Without letting go, she moves us out into the hall, to another room past the open bathroom.

Wow.

Books.

Lots of books.

She can read?

"You see what I had to do to get you back?" She unlatches me and walks to the middle of the room. "All these damn books. Every single one I read, and they weren't fuckin' easy either." She waves her hand across the top of one bookcase. "These are all huge and over a thousand-pages, written over a hundred years ago. I had to learn a new language. I had to learn to do *magic*. Magic, Drew. Not a pissant's birthday party BS, but real, honest-to-God, magic."

I gloss over the bindings. Many are in obscure languages; others are too faded to read; some don't have titles. She continues on about magic… There's so many that I can't understand how she afforded them. Some look older than my grandparents, my grandparents' grandparents. Probably stole them or money to buy them.

"… And I brought you back, Drew. *I* did; no one else. No one called or asked about you after the accident, but I loved you enough to collect all the parts and put you back together."

I don't understand. What the hell is she talking about? Putting me back together? Collecting parts? Is she more batshit than she was that night at the bar? Is that possible? Only a crazy bitch would drug a stranger and keep him captive in her house, but now she's apparently a magician.

"Aren't you impressed?" she says, hands on hips.

I stare at her for a moment, two, and I force a smile and nod. Mouth, "Thank you."

When she started downstairs, I pointed to my groin and eventually she understood I had to piss, but didn't really. She stands outside the closed door. Peeling linoleum floor, urine-yellow walls, a stained toilet caddy corner with a rusted tub, a mirror above the sink, nearly opaque with dried toothpaste.

I search under the sink. No tweezers or anything sharp. I pull out the narrow drawers above and there's wet wipes, tampons, and a variety of condoms.

I go to open the medicine cabinet behind the mirror—

Holy.

Those aren't my eyes. This isn't my nose. These aren't my lips or ears, or even my hair. This isn't my fucking face.

I try to recollect what I looked like before the crash but it's foggy, vague. I can picture settings and scenes, but not myself or people. Like a diorama without the figurines. But I'm *sure* my eyes looked less… crazy? Wild? They sure as hell weren't green. And, my nose was narrower, my lips were thinner and my ears were definitely not this small… And my hair, my hair was dark brown, and I'm nearer to reddish-blonde than anything.

"Everythin' okay there?" Terry calls through the door.

I let out a deaf noise. She doesn't reply.

I scramble out of my clothes. Really look at myself for the first time since waking up.

My left leg is noticeably shorter than my right; my right is far more muscular than my left and—holy shit my dick wasn't *this* big—stomach's tanner than my thighs and chest—is my chest shallower?—arms are two different shades, extremely pale, orangish; and a faded tattoo of some wavy symbol is on my right shoulder—I raise my hands. One has wrinkles, the other doesn't. The lines across the palms are different, too.

I stare wide-eyed at my reflection.

Who—what am I?

What the *fuck* happened to me?

I open my mouth. My teeth seem the same but who could tell if they weren't? She's right though. My tongue's gone. Not cut out, it's simply not there. Lean in, find my tonsils are gone, too. I *know* I didn't get those out, because I was the only one of my friends who didn't growing up.

I'm shivering.

Dry-cry.

There's a pounding in the back of my skull that rattles my spine.

I collapse onto the toilet, put my face in my hands.

What did she *do* to me?

Terry pounds on the door, so I flush the toilet, get dressed and go out. I wanted to smash her into the floor. I wanted to squeeze her skull until brain matter came out her nose. But I was weak, exhausted. I yawned and she said, "You sleepy, honey?"

I nodded.

She took me back to her bedroom, pushed off the heap of clothes hiding the mattress on the floor. "You can sleep here. I'm not tired yet, so I'mma go downstairs. Prepare for tomorrow."

She hugged and kissed me, tucked me in, and turned off the lights before closing the door. The lock clicked into place.

Moonlight shines through the window as I stare aimlessly at the popcorn ceiling. Sift through my mind like endless rows of featureless sheets hung out to dry. Can't find anything. Every time I pull back one, there's another, and another, and then there's a blank spot where something should be.

But... Vaguely, I remember the night I met Terry, at some bar. I was passing through town for something... I walked from somewhere, upset for a reason that's lost to me, and found the nearest, cheapest bar. Few drinks deep, Terry came over, started feeding me shots... Went to the bathroom at some point, came back, took another shot and... I can still taste the way the whiskey was bitter, almost sour, despite being without a tongue.

And, there, another memory appears.

Sitting on the porch with Terry in the morning. I just woke up. Very groggy. Tongue heavy and furry. We talked about something, and she pushed over a cup of coffee. I thought my black out was from the drinking. Thought the coffee was an odd flavor she liked, like rum cake or walnut cream, but before I could finish the cup I was out like a light.

Days or weeks, I have no clue, when I came to in a windowless room, on a bed with no sheets or pillows. A pile of trash in the corner by a heap of hamburger helper on a paper plate; in the opposite corner was a plastic bucket by a standing lamp and the closed door.

A blank spot, then:

Hammering the door, screaming for Terry, for anyone to get me the hell out. The hamburger helper splattered against the wall, meat and brown sauce and noodles running onto the hard carpet.

Blank spot.

On the bed, hands raised, warding off Terry as she pointed a pistol at me. She's screaming. I'm pleading to not be killed, to be let go. Her words muffled noises, but: "Why the hell would you want to leave? We love each other, right? It's fuckin' fate! You don't leave the ones your soulmate," breaks through.

More screaming. She leaves and—

My heart slams against my chest. I grip the blankets. I want the release of crying. I want the release of pain and helplessness but they're trapped inside me like I am in this damn house.

The window's appealing but it's a two-story drop, and Terry probably nailed it shut.

I have to get the hell out of here.

The kitchen is almost spotless when she calls me down. She cleaned and put away the dishes, wiped down the counter, and mopped the floor. On the gleaning table, several paper plates of breakfast foods: eggs, bacon, pancakes, and sausages. Hazelnut lingers in the air, and the coffee pot hisses.

She sits at the table with her hands on the vinyl, smiling. Bags under her eyes. She must've been up all night doing this.

"See baby, I worked hard for you. Sit, sit, eat. You need your strength."

I want to tell her I don't think I can eat without a tongue, don't think I'm *built* to eat anymore, but I don't want to have a one-sided argument. So, I grab a plate and take a scoop of each food. She places a mug of coffee next to me as I sit, and I stare at it for a couple seconds, then take it, too. What the hell's the point of worrying now?

I eat the eggs first—probably the safest choice—and after chewing them thoroughly, I force a swallow. I cough, not all went down, and gulp the coffee. Can't burn the tongue I don't have.

The warm liquid and eggs slide down my throat, plop into my stomach like rocks. It doesn't feel right instantly, like those things aren't meant to be there, inside me.

"How is it—" she begins, but I sprint upstairs to the bathroom, vomiting into the toilet. Brownish eggs and phlegmy dark liquid fills the bowl. I sit back, relieved, and wipe the slime from my lips.

That settles that. Can't eat either, which begs the question even more: What the hell am I? Can't eat or drink, can barely sleep; can't feel my groin and, I assume, can't piss or shit or orgasm. I'm like a mannequin with a heartbeat and working lungs.

Terry appears in the doorway, wide-eyed. "You okay? Everythin' all right? I made sure I cooked those eggs through. Must've been a bad batch or somethin'."

Or, you created a monster and are trying to make it into something it's not.

She helps me up and we go back downstairs. She takes me into the living room and sets me down into an old recliner. Terry returns to the kitchen. The news plays on the TV. A female newscaster is going on about something I don't care about. The date in the corner reads: *July 22, 2009.*

Two-thousand nine?

Holy shit… It's been *three* years? Three years that's a blank spot in my mind. Was I dead? Did I die in that accident? Or was I in a coma? A vegetable? I shake my head. Can't be. If I were, I would've had the same body as I did before… So, I died; must've. If that's the case… How the hell am I here? How did she do all this? Bring me here? Give me life? Was she being serious about using magic? Is there *actually* magic?

I sit back, exhale…

I… I just… Too much is happening at once and I'm so lost in my own head. I'm dead, but not, a zombie without the urge to eat flesh, a vampire disinterested in blood; I'm imprisoned here; there's magic in the world and someone like Terry can use it. My previous life feels like someone else's, and the few memories I do have are insignificant.

OK…

OK…

"Fah-awk," I say, forcing myself to focus on anything else. Slowly the terror blotting my mind dissipates. All these things aren't important currently. Escaping from this house, from Terry, is. When I'm far away and safe, I'll deal with the questions.

My heart slows, calming.

Another thought: If this body isn't mine, are the organs not mine, either?

Let's not think about that…

We sit on the back porch. She's smoking a cigarette. The patchy, brown grass overcomes the cracked walkway midway in the yard. A metal fence surrounds us, and beyond an alleyway with a few houses on the opposite side. I mentally note everything. Will probably need it soon.

"So what was it like?"

I raise an eyebrow.

"Bein' gone?" She twirls the cigarette in the air. "Like, the other side and all that?"

I shrug. Doesn't she remember I can't talk?

"Did it feel good?"

I shake my head.

"Bad?"

Shake my head.

"Then what?"

I shrug again.

She grumbles, takes a drag, pushes it out. "You feel any different than before?"

I have no idea, and shrug, again.

"Jesus Christ, don't you know anythin' Drew? I do all this shit for you and you can't even fuckin' tell me if it was worth it."

I have no idea what she wants me to say, so I put my hand onto her lower back and rub. I don't want to fight. Must keep her content. She smiles, leans into it. "Oh baby, that feels *good*."

No cars parked in the alley, or in the gravel driveways. No bikes or motorcycles either. There's a few trashcans about. Might be something I can use in one of them.

"Don't stop," she says and I realize I have, start round two.

We stay like this until she finishes off three cigarettes, and she goes inside to prepare my 'favorite meal.'

God only knows what that is.

With the quiet of the neighborhood and the growing evening, I feel something like peace. Crickets begin chirping. Fireflies appear. A cool breeze blows. Nostalgia washes over me but I can't understand why. It's aggravating—I want to know *what* the hell she did to me.

"Drew!" Terry calls from the house, and I breathe in deep, push the anger down as much as I can. "Drew, food's ready."

I stand and go inside. Wander through the empty kitchen, living room, and go upstairs to find her in the bedroom. She's nude and her legs are spread at the edge of the bed.

"Dinner's ready," she grins.

She's asleep next to me in the dark. Once more, I'm back staring at the popcorn ceiling. I completed the act without a tongue—it was more of motorboating than anything close to oral sex. At least she cleaned and shaved beforehand.

I let an hour, two, pass, and gently slide the blanket back and sneak out of bed. Tiptoe into the hallway, down the stairs, to the kitchen. I don't want to simply escape. I want to ruin her. Destroy her. Take her apart and never put her back together. She took my life, my seemingly death, and afterlife. My memories. My dreams. Everything that I was or could be. The bitch played God.

I pull open a drawer. A bunch of junk. Close it and open another, and another, until the narrow one by the fridge is open, revealing knives. Tons of them. Must've bought them at a yard sale or something because none of them match. I take the thinnest, sharpest one I can find, and close the drawer.

I'm dry sweating.

This is it.

I creep back into the bedroom.

She's still on her side, facing the wall, in bed. Snoring.

I can't help but smile. I can't help but be excited, like a kid coming downstairs on Christmas morning.

I gently lie back down, roll over, and bring the knife up.

Take her heart, like she did mine—

"You better put that knife down Drew, or so help me God you'll be kissin' the ceilin'," she rolls onto her back, eyes open. A gun in her hand, the barrel poking out from the blanket, shoved under my chin. She must keep it under the mattress.

Our gaze remain locked.

"Drop it, lover."

I do. It falls onto her stomach. She brushes it to the floor. "Lay on your back."

I listen.

"I don't understand why you would want to hurt me, baby, after all I've done." She nestles into my side, forces my arm over her. "You wouldn't have any of this without me. You would be nothin' but bits in the dirt."

I peer over her head. Knife's nowhere in sight.

"I'll let this one go, though. People fuck up sometimes. It's fine. Just gotta' get back on the wagon and keep goin'."

Silence…

"But if you try that shit again, no matter how much I love you, I will take you out. Then, I'll bring you back and we can try again because we're meant to be. We'll keep tryin' and tryin' and some day things'll work out."

A repeating life of this. Of Terry. Of dying and rebirth and dying and rebirth, praying to stay in one place but being pulled into the other. Of peace torn away and thrown into the pits with this crazy woman. Terry and brimstone.

Plans immediately change, flipping from one to another.

I only need to escape her, not kill her, or harm her. She's seemingly untouchable in her home. I need to get somewhere far away, and attack her when she doesn't expect it. In an alley when she's grocery shopping, after she leaves a bar; anywhere, doing anything.

Faintly, I wonder if I will age… If I do nothing, I could wait her out. Doubt it.

"You hear me, *Drew*? You listenin'?"

I nod, pull her closer.

"That's a good boy…" She yawns. "Let's get back to sleep."

A scream echoes in my head.

She locked me in the library, said she had to run errands. I already tried the knob, tried pulling on the door but it didn't budge.

I run my finger along the book spines. A partial memory forms of being young, walking down the library's aisles, inspecting the titles, searching for my next adventure. But reading these books' back covers, they're obscure and esoteric, like a madman's ravings about different worlds and gods and other bullshit.

I pull a narrow one down, open it to a random page, skim it.

Yup. Exactly what I thought.

Shelve it, move along to the next shelf, and the other. My fingers rest on a thick untitled book. It looks like the one Terry held when I woke up in the basement.

I remove it, turn to the front page, and sit on the floor. It has a variety of ink illustrations of glyphs and runes, and text-ridden brittle pages of rituals, enchantments, and so forth. I flip through until I come upon the wavy symbol that matches the one on my shoulder, the same on the metal table.

Conventus Renascentiae-avium

What the hell…

It's in Latin, but there's some English words. I don't understand how Terry could read this, let alone pronounce it. Words stand out like *assemble, innards, conduit, Phoenix*. I get the gist of it once I finish the page. It's some sort of ritual to bring back someone from the dead, Frankenstein-ing them back together from parts of other people.

I close the book, set it aside, and press my hand to my stomach, probing organs, pinch my ribs and sternum. Run my hand over my chest, my neck, push fingers through hair.

I have my answer.

I'm me but not me.

It raises another horrifying question: How'd she get the parts?

I stand as the door unlocks and swings open.

"You have fun?" she says.

I shrug, smile. Have to give her something.

"Well that's good," her accent makes *good* sound like *ga-uhd*. "C'mon down stairs, I gotta' surprise."

My feet don't want to move, but I force them. Cold fear ascends my spine, settling below my hair. Down the stairs, through the kitchen with bagged groceries on the counter and table, the hallway, to the living room.

Stop.

"You like it?"

A TV. A big, flat TV. I wonder how much it costs, how she could pay for it. From what I know, she has no job. It stands on the old wooden one. Two TVs. Christ…

I nod.

"I saw it while I was out. It was on sale! I thought: Hey, I have a man in the house now. He'll want a bigger TV to watch the games on when football season starts."

I walk to it, and consider picking it up and smashing it over her head, but she's probably packing heat. Instead, run my fingers up the side, find and press the power button.

The black screen fades to an image of the news. I stand back, Terry next to me wraps her arm under mine.

"Pretty, ain't it?"

I don't nod or mouth anything, and watch the newscaster go on about something in the Middle East.

I'm out of my body, suddenly—experiencing the world through a window. Terry's touch revolts me but it's like I'm wearing a layer of plastic. Can feel it, but incompletely. Her arm around a stranger's. Everything's surreal, fake. I'm uncomfortable, but aware it's happening because of what I learned in the books.

And, maybe… that this is all there will be forever.

This will be my life but not my life.

With Terry. With this stupidly huge TV. A fucked up modern family. She'll ask for kids at some point, force me to try to knock her up despite the lack of semen.

I recall what depression, hopelessness felt like years ago and this is similar, wanting to melt into the floor and allow my being to soak into the carpet, the wood, the earth, until I am nothing but sustenance for the worms…

No.

I can't.

She's only a person smart enough to trap me and read old texts. Maybe I believe she's smarter than she is. Maybe what I think to be two steps ahead is pure luck. Maybe I'm *over*estimating her.

I'll get out of this. I'll leave this damn place. But the question: *Then what?* forms, and I push it aside. I'll worry about that when I get there.

Terry left me in the recliner to enjoy the gift. She's in the kitchen, preparing dinner. The smell of meatloaf and pungent spices slither into the room. The stove closes with a clash.

I stare aimlessly at whatever's on. A plan. I need a plan more than anything else. The doors are locked, and the windows—I'll have to look— are likely nailed shut. She sleeps with me at night, and is with me most of the day, except when she has to run errands. But, she locks me in there, which has no windows… or does it? One of the bookcases may be blocking one… I'll check tomorrow.

The basement doesn't have windows or a doorway to the yard. If it does have the former, they're slatted and near the ceiling, like most basements. Too risky to go down there on my own anyway, but if the opportunity arises—

"Dinner's almost ready, baby!" she hollers.

I wave my hand as though she can see it.

—And, although I want a plan for what happens when I get out, there's too many options to decide on. The easiest one is to simply run, run as far and fast as I can anywhere and do whatever as things come. If I find a police station, go to it; if I find help, use it; if someone wants to give me a ride into a town over, take it.

I absentmindedly pick up the remote, switching channels. Smoke stains the air.

"Oh shit! Shit, shit, shit!" The stove clangs open, slams closed. Glass slides across the steel grates. Blowing, whipping of a towel. "Fuck, fuck, fuck—okay, we're okay. We're okay, baby! Dinner's done!"

At sunrise, Terry woke me and put me into the library, locking the door. Errands, apparently. Which sucked because it was one of the few nights I was able to sleep. No dreams I can recall, and that disappointments me, yet relieves me. What could I dream of? Would I dream of the people I'm made from? Dream of the place between life and death?

Yawning, I rub my eyes, and stretch. Yawn again. Soon I'm fully present and begin with the bookcase on the right. Drag it out, careful to not spill any of the books. There's a bare yellow wall behind it.

Move the one against the left wall. Again, nothing.

The one against the far wall is heavier, larger, and it takes me a while of carefully nudging and pulling, walking it towards me, to create enough space behind it. I slide between the crevice of the right bookshelf and peek behind the far wall one…

Eyes widen.

A window!

It's covered by a black curtain, but the nicked wooden frame pokes out. I gently push the bookshelf out more, more, more… Enough room for me to shimmy through, with my face turned against the wall.

It's tight, but I manage to pull the curtain open, peer out. The window leads to the porch roof, and it looks like a couple feet to the front yard. My legs aren't my own, but I hope they're sturdy enough for the drop. I'm tingling and giddy, excited.

Wait!

Wait…

I pry back the rusted lock on the window, wrench it open with one hand.

It opens! Yes! A cold breeze wafts in, raising goosebumps on my arm. I smell garbage, but I don't care, it's welcome. I want to run… Why don't I?

I jam my fingers under the window screen, pop it loose, but as I lift, a Sedan pulls into the drive alongside the house. I halt. Watch… Terry gets out.

Shit. Quickly, quietly, close the screen and window, re-curtain it, and slide out from behind the bookcase.

I hear the front door open and close.

I push the larger bookshelf back, shove the others into place. Stand back. They look the same. She won't be able to tell unless she inspects them closely.

Footsteps on the stairs.

But will she?

Is she that smart or am I overestimating her again?

I shove the two side bookshelves again. Arrange some books that moved.

The lock clicks behind me and I turn to greet Terry while she opens the door.

"Mornin' sunshine," she's carrying a cardboard carrier with two coffees and from the sugary scent, a bag of doughnuts. "Ready for breakfast?"

I can't stop thinking about the window. The cold air on my skin. The smell of trash. The openness. The freedom. I only know being trapped here. This feeling is new, as though I'm reborn. I imagine grass and flowers, trees and vines, valleys and plains and creeks and rivers and—

"You sure you don't want any, babe?" Terry says through a mouthful of doughnut holes, as we sit at the kitchen table.

I shake my head, smile. I wave my hand, signifying: "Go ahead, you have them."

She shrugs, plops another in her mouth and sips her second coffee.

Knees shaking. Hands prickly. I want to run, leap, fly. But can't, not yet. Have to take it slow, have patience. Jumping the gun would fuck everything up. I realize I'm biting my nails—a habit I never had before. Terry does, too. "You okay, babe?"

I mouth: "Fine."

I sit in the living room. The news plays loudly on TV. Terry's upstairs taking a bath. As I hear the water slosh as she gets in, it hits me that this is the moment I've been waiting for. I'm thrown off because of the unexpectedness of it… I was preparing for a week or two from today, but it's here. I'm unattended, completely, for the first time.

I go to the stairs, listen… Water spilling on the floor, her whistling. I rush to the backdoor in the kitchen, it's safer: the bathroom partially faces the front yard, if my memories are right. Adrenaline floods someone's veins. I fumble with the locks. Briefly wonder how this is so easy, but ignore it. She's Terry. A dumbass. Probably didn't think I would run anyway.

I step outside, barefoot—Big smile. The cold feels amazing. I'm free! I run down the walkway, cut through wet grass, and climb over the steel fence. The gravel alley bites into my feet but I can't be bothered to care. At the end of the alley: right or left? Right. There's no cars or people out. Debris litters the pavement, plasters the bottom of unlit street lights. Street drains congested with trash. The intersection light creaks as the wind moves it. Turning at the street corner, I pass by a spray-painted stop sign.

Start sprinting all out.

"Didn't read that part, huh, dumb shit?" a voice says in the nothingness of unconsciousness. "Wake up, Drew." My eyes flutter open.

Encircled by hazy darkness, Terry stands over me, damp hair tied back. The sodium street lamp gives her an orange-yellow aura.

How long has it been?

Where am I?

Why are my insides on fire, my limbs searing, gasoline igniting my marrow?

Crossing the street, running. Legs becoming tired, exhausted... Coming undone at the hips. I stumble as something inside cracks and splits. Crash to the ground, cry out, but dig my nails into the cement and drag myself forward. My lower back unhinges, my neck weakens and my head drags across the sidewalk. I give up crawling and roll into the grass ditch and ragdoll down into some bushes. There's popping and I can't feel my arms anymore. What the hell is happening? drums in my head. One eye goes black. The other. My jaw slackens and numbs. No, no, no...

Terry kneels, slaps my leg. "I know you read the book, but you musta' missed a chapter." I realize she has the book in her arm. She opens it.

"I'm not goin' to read word-for-word," she skims the page, "because this shit is hard understanding, let alone speakin'." She peers over the text down at me. "But, the gist is that you can only go so far from where you came from or you'll come apart." She closes the book, tucks it under her arm. "So you can't leave Drew. You're stuck to me like flies on shit forever, like we're supposed to be, baby."

She straightens. The stars are out above her, and I desperately want more than anything for them to fall and incinerate my existence. If I could feel my mouth, I'd let out a deaf moan.

"Let's get your ass back home."

Home.

Home…

Despite not having one, I know in my bones this isn't my home.

These walls, the popcorn ceiling, the bed under me. The limbs and organs and flesh. Everything that I am isn't me. I am a structure, like the house. I am not a person but a puzzle mashed together until it became whole. I'm not meant to be here, alive, existent. An abomination. A monster. Is this how Frankenstein's Creature felt? Must've been. At least he wasn't imprisoned by someone like Terry…

"You doin' okay, babe?" Terry says from the doorway.

I nod.

"Good. You should be done healin' in a day or two, then you'll be right as rain."

Wonderful.

She goes downstairs. I hear the TV come on.

Am I the one with the problem?

Am *I* the problem?

Would someone else accept this for what it is? It doesn't look as bad from the outside. Stuck with a woman who adores him, a woman who brought her love by to—

Stop!

Don't think like that. Don't *ever* think like that. She defiled your body in all ways possible. She's tethered you to her, her house, her life. You are a victim in all aspects, and by the power of some supernatural bullshit, you'll forever be one as long as you miserably live.

The first option is back on the table. Can't leave. Can't die, as far as I'm aware. She has to go as soon as possible. I will make her home into mine, like she made me into something she believes is hers.

A week passes by in a blur, and I'm good as new. All feeling in my limbs, toes, and fingers is back. I can yawn, mouth words, and look around. We sit in the kitchen in the morning. Terry's drinking a strawberry smoothie and I idly stare at the table. A cool breeze blows in through the open window above the sink. Birds chirp.

"So whatchu' wanna watch today?" She takes a gulp of the pink slush.

I shrug.

"Pick somethin'."

I don't know. I don't care. Shrug again.

"For fuck's sake, Drew. Be a man and be somethin', do somethin'. I can't be makin' all the decisions."

But you *chose* this. You *decided* this. You're God and I'm Adam. You tell me where to go, I go; tell me to stand, I do; tell me go down on you, I do. Can't bitch about something you did to yourself.

Shrug.

She finishes her drink, gets up and tosses the cup in the sink. "Jesus Christ. I didn't think you'd be such a pussy. Maybe I shouldn't've brought you back." She spits, literally, pink-tinged phlegm hitting me.

I clench my hands, pressing nails into doughy palms.

"You gonna say somethin'? Do somethin'?" She leans in, hands flat on the table. Her hair hangs over her face like dirty rags. "Or you just gonna sit there like a little bitch?"

Something like blood seeps between fingernails, trickles onto my jeans. I feel like I'm shaking and realize I actually am.

Our sight locks.

"Oh, someone's mad now. That's a first." She closes in, noses almost touching. She's grinning. She thinks this is a game. Foreplay, like the porn she watches sometimes at night. She's into men taking what they want. Angry sex, hate fucking. "Whatta' gonna do Drew? Huh?"

This isn't fake. This rage is *real*. And, the single thing I want to do in my life is take hers.

Before she realizes what's happening, I spring forward and grab her neck. Fingers dig into her throat while my other arm wraps around her waist and I'm rising, her with me, then slamming her down onto the table. I burrow nails into her windpipe. My hand leaps from her waist to join the other, squeezing her esophagus closed.

It feels so easy.

It feels like this was meant to happen years ago.

I'm surprisingly strong.

Why hadn't I done this before?

Was it because I didn't want to kill?

Was it because I didn't want to be the monster she created?

No, no, no… *Terry's* the monster. She made me into this.

She's kicking out but her knees are bent and her feet weakly hit my legs. Arms flailing, fingernails scratching my arms and face. Tears dribble down her blueing cheeks, soaking hair splayed out under her. I press harder. Her teeth clench between purpling lips. Wide eyes bulging.

The table's legs give out, it collapses underneath us and we crash to the floor. I lose my grip. She's on her stomach, kicking out, scrambling towards the hallway. Coughing. Hacking. I reach for her ankle but she heels my jaw, sending me reeling. I rub my chin, shaking my head, stand and trudge towards her as she hobbles towards the stairs, going for the gun in her bedroom.

"Stop! Please, baby!" she screams as I throw her by her hair to the floor. Hunkering over her, pinning her clawing hands to the hardwood, I press my knees onto her arms. She knees my groin but I feel nothing. Finally it works out for me.

Hair plasters her sweaty beet-red face. I take her neck into my hands once more, and put all my weight into it, as though I'm pressing her into the fibers of the wood.

"Dr… ew," she sputters through puckered lips. "Pl… se… D… n't."

Her knees stop, legs give up.

"P… e… B… be… I… ve… ou…"

Veins bulge against her temples. Joints wail as I press my fingers as deep as her skin allows.

"… ease… Dr—"

Her eyes roll into the back of her head, revealing pinkish whites.

A gasp escapes her, a waft of strawberry breath, and her chest rattles… Stops. And, even then after the reek of shit and piss stain the air, I don't let go… The sunlight coming through the sink window brightens. More birds begin chirping. Cars start and there's some chatter outside from the unseen neighbors.

I pry my stiff fingers from her, revealing deeply bruised indents. My legs weak, I give up on standing and fall back onto my ass.

I can't believe it.

Can't fucking believe.

It's over, actually *over*.

Relief, sadness; happiness, and despair collide and wash over me. I smile while dry-sobbing into my hands.

Even though I'm finally free, I'm still trapped.

. . .

I don't bury her. She doesn't deserve it.

In the square, gray basement, I discover the steel door behind the freezer on wheels. Doesn't take a genius to figure out it was there; how many freezers are on wheels?

Undo the latch, open it. Passing the hanging plastic sheets, I enter the freezing room.

My birthplace.

I find the light switch, flick it on. Harsh light blares, gleaning off the metal table scarred with the weird symbols matching my shoulder tattoo. A huge blackened purple crystal hangs above it, charred nubs stick out. The symbols on the walls and floor are burnt, too.

Nostalgia overwhelms me. Like somewhere I hate but unknowingly long for. It's strangely bittersweet. Could this room be considered my childhood home? My mother? Her womb? I know nothing else.

I turn to the doorway.

Because of *her*.

I left Terry on the basement floor. I heave her over my shoulder, carry her inside, and lay her down onto the table. This'll be her tomb of irony. She'll remain in the place where she brought back something that shouldn't have been. A cement placenta of beginnings and ends.

I turn the light off on the way out, lock the steel door, and push the freezer back in place.

Outside in the afternoon light, I stand on the front porch. The house needs work but I seemingly have all the time in the world. I will make it my own, like she did me. Discover the boundaries and limitations of my freedom. Get Internet installed, buy a computer, find where she must store her cash, and purchase as many books as I can and read, research, study; learn and perhaps break the fucking tether binding me here, and go wherever— become whoever—I want.

Hopefully one day, soon.

AFTERWORD

Thanks to the folks at *D&T Publishing* for believing in this book, and all the help they've provided making it the best it can be. Also want to thank all the editors who've helped me more than they could know to get me to this point. I appreciate everything you all have done, even the rejections.

Many thanks to JT, JD, and the Kids. You were always supportive and even though I don't show it, I appreciate it.

Another thanks to the horror community, primarily on Twitter, for always being there and being supportive to every writer, big or small. I can't remember everyone, but those who I've spoken with over the years deserve their own mention (in no particular order): Orrin Grey, Gwendolyn Kiste, Sara Tantlinger, RJ Murrary, Scott J. Moses, Kyle Winklier, Matt Wildasin, Matthew Stott, Robert Ottone, Sam Richard, Mike Davis, Joe Koch, Patrick Barb, Sarah Budd, and so many others. And one last, special mention to HWA Pittsburgh, no one could ask for a better group.

MICAH CASTLE

About the Author

Micah Castle is a weird fiction and horror writer. His stories have appeared in various magazines, websites, and anthologies. He has three collections and one novella currently out.

While away from the keyboard, he enjoys spending time with his wife, being in the woods, playing with his animals, and can typically be found reading a book somewhere in his Pennsylvania home.

Contact him at https://www.micahcastle.com or https://twitter.com/Micah_Castle

ABOUT THE EDITOR / PUBLISHER

Dawn Shea is an author and half of the publishing team over at D&T Publishing. She lives with her family in Mississippi. Always an avid horror lover, she has moved forward with her dreams of writing and publishing those things she loves so much.

D&T Previously published material:
    ABC's of Terror
    After the Kool-Aid is Gone

Follow her author page on Amazon for all publications she is featured in.
    Follow D&T Publishing at the following locations:
    Website
    Facebook: Page / Group
    Or email us here: dandtpublishing20@gmail.com

Reconstructing A Relationship by Micah Castle

Edited by Jimmy Heideker

Cover by Don Noble

Formatting by J.Z. Foster

Corinth, MS